Jill Dow trained at the Royal College of Art.
Since graduating she has worked as a freelance illustrator
specialising in natural history, including the highly successful series
Bellamy's Changing World for Frances Lincoln. The *Windy Edge Farm* stories
have become bestsellers and have been published in many different
countries and languages. Jill is passionate about gardening and the
countryside and is a regular contributor to national gardening publications.
She lives near Stirling in Scotland with her husband and
their three children.

The Windy Edge Farm Series:
Webster's Walk,
Maggie's Holiday,
Molly's Supper,
Bridget's Secret,
Hazel and Clover's Great Escape
Hepzibah's Woolly Fleece,
Piggy Little's Hide and Seek,
Moonbeam's Big Splash.

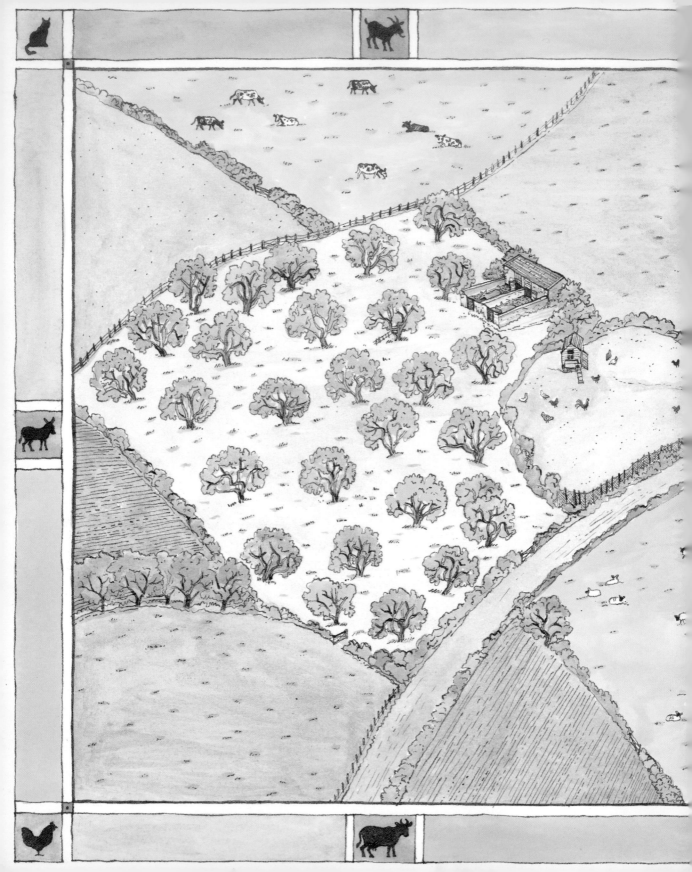

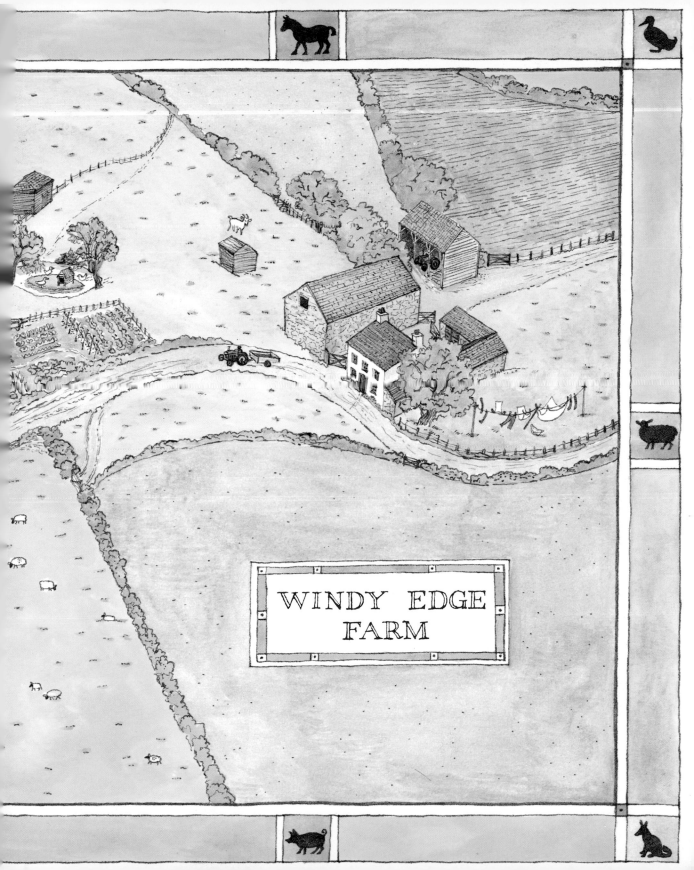

WINDY EDGE
FARM

*For Jake, Leon
and Charlie*

First published in Great Britain in 1989 by
Frances Lincoln Limited, 4 Torriano Mews,
Torriano Avenue, London NW5 2RZ

British Library Cataloguing in Publication Data available on request

ISBN 0-7112-1780-7

Printed in Hong Kong

3 5 7 9 8 6 4 2

Design and art direction   Debbie MacKinnon

WINDY EDGE FARM

Bridget's Secret

Jill Dow

to Joy, with best wishes from
Jill Dow

FRANCES LINCOLN

Angus liked all the hens at Windy Edge Farm, but his favourite was Bridget. She was a little black hen with a bright red comb that sat on top of her head like a little hat. Whenever Angus visited the henhouse, Bridget ran clucking to meet him and pecked softly at his feet until he sat down on the step. Then she would hop into his lap and let him stroke her smooth shiny feathers.

Bridget liked to be different. Every morning, all the other hens laid their eggs in the laying boxes inside the henhouse, before going outside to scratch for food.

But Bridget liked to go outside first, and lay her brown speckled egg in a different place every day.

Angus always had to hunt high and low to find Bridget's egg.
On Monday, it was inside the dog's kennel.

On Tuesday, Bridget laid it in the goatshed.

On Wednesday Angus found it in the pigsty, and only just saved it from being eaten by one of Sarah's piglets.

On Thursday it was hidden under a tree in the orchard,

and on Friday it was in the barn, tucked
between the folds of the old woolly jumper
that Molly used as her bed.

But on Saturday, Angus couldn't find Bridget's
egg anywhere. Nor could he find Bridget. He
called her name, and hunted in all her favourite
places, but the little black hen was nowhere to
be seen.

Then, just as he was ready to give up, Angus heard a strange clucking sound coming from under the rhubarb. He got down on his hands and knees to have a look under the huge leaves – and there was Bridget. But for once she didn't seem at all pleased to see him. She fluffed out her feathers until she looked twice as big as usual, and made angry clucking noises when he tried to touch her. Was she ill? Or had the fox frightened her in the night?

Angus ran to tell his mother about Bridget's strange behaviour, but she laughed and told him not to worry.

"Bridget is BROODY," she said. "She wants to sit on some eggs until they hatch into baby chicks. We'll have to make her a nice warm nest."

So next day, when Angus had collected the eggs from the hens in the henhouse, he didn't take them all indoors to be made into cakes or custard or scrambled egg. Instead, he put six of them carefully on the soft nest of straw that his mother had made inside an old barrel. Then he fetched Bridget and sat her on the nest, tucking her own speckled egg in with the other six under her warm feathers.

Every morning, Angus brought fresh
food and water for Bridget,

and every afternoon he watched the
clutch of eggs while she left the nest
for a few minutes

to stretch
her legs

and wings.

One week went by, then another. Would the eggs never hatch?

"Be patient," said his mother. "Bridget knows what she's doing."

The days of the third week dragged slowly by.
"I don't believe there *are* any chickens inside
those eggs," thought Angus sadly.

But on Sunday morning Angus found the barrel empty. Bridget had gone, and in the straw lay the cracked and empty shells of seven eggs.

Angus was very upset. He thought the fox must have eaten Bridget and all her eggs, and as he ran to tell his mother, he began to cry.

But just as he was running through the
vegetable patch, he heard a low gentle clucking,
and a soft high-pitched cheeping.
Angus stopped and listened carefully.
Could it be Bridget?

Angus parted the leaves, and was thrilled to find his favourite hen, safe and sound with seven little chicks nestling close to her.

One of the chicks looked different from the others – she had little dark patches on her fluffy feathers.

When she saw Angus,
she left her mother and
came running to meet him,
pecking at his new shoes
with her tiny beak. This one,
Angus decided, was going to
be just like Bridget!

– The End –

MORE TITLES IN PAPERBACK
FROM THE WINDY EDGE FARM SERIES
BY JILL DOW

WEBSTER'S WALK

When the summer sun dries up the duck pond,
Webster leads a possie of ducks in search of the river.

ISBN 0-7112-1777-7

MOLLY'S SUPPER

Molly has been out hunting all day, but hasn't caught
a single thing. A long way from home and already late for
her supper, she hurries back. Will she get home in time?

ISBN 0-7112-1776-9

MAGGIE'S HOLIDAY

When old Mr McNab goes away to visit his son in Australia,
Maggie the pony is lonely. But one night a terrible storm
destroys her stable and changes her life forever.

ISBN 0-7112-1778-5

*The Windy Edge Farm series is suitable for National Curriculum English — Reading,
Key Stage 1 and Scottish Guidelines English Language — Reading, Level B*

Frances Lincoln titles are available from all good bookshops.